JACK KENT

PIGGY BANK
GONZALES

Parents' Magazine Press · New York

Library of Congress Cataloging in Publication Data

Kent, Jack, 1920–   Piggy Bank Gonzales.
Summary: A piggy bank, bored with the sameness of every day, discovers
that life outside his quiet Mexican home can be too exciting.
[1. Coin banks—Fiction. 2. Mexico—Fiction] I. Title.   PZ7.K414Pi
ISBN 0-8193-0997-4   ISBN 0-8193-0998-2 lib. bdg.

Para mis amigos mejicanos

In a little house
in a little town in Mexico
there was a piggy bank.
It belonged to a family
named Gonzales.

Piggy Bank Gonzales
led a quiet life.
Every day Mama Gonzales
dusted him off and gave him
a loving pat on the head.

Now and then
one of the Gonzales children
dropped a coin through the slot
on his back.
Then they would shake him
to rattle the coins
so they could try to guess
how many there were.

But most of the time he just sat
on a table near the window
and watched the people go by.

It was a pleasant life.
A comfortable life.
But not very exciting.

"It's boring!"
said Piggy Bank Gonzales.
He wanted adventure.

One day a pig walked by
playing a violin.
That was more than
Piggy Bank Gonzales could resist.
"Wait for me!" he cried.

He jumped out of the window
and ran after the pig
with the violin.

"I'm a pig, too,"
said Piggy Bank Gonzales.

"Pooh!" snorted the pig.
"You aren't a real pig, like me!
You're only made of clay!"
And he walked off
with his snout in the air.

The piggy bank followed
on behind.

They met a pig with a guitar.
They met another with a trumpet.
The three pig musicians
played a happy tune.

Other pigs began to dance.

"I can dance, too,"
said Piggy Bank Gonzales.
He joined the dancers.

"Who is that?"
asked one of the pigs.

"Just a clay pig,"
answered another.

"Make him go away!"
said a third.

But Piggy Bank Gonzales
went on dancing.
As he danced the coins inside him
jingled merrily.

A few coins popped out
of the slot in his back.
They bounced and rolled
on the ground.

"Money!" shouted the pigs.
"The clay pig is rich!"
They ran hither and thither
chasing the coins.

"Let's go to market!" they cried.
And off they ran.

At the market each of the pigs
chose a big hat for himself.

Piggy Bank Gonzales tried
to choose a hat, too.
But the pigs got in his way.

When it was time
to pay for the hats
the musicians began to play.
"Dance, piggy bank," they said.

Piggy Bank Gonzales danced.
Coins popped out of the slot
on his back.
Soon there were enough
to pay the bill.

Next each of the pigs
chose a fancy blanket
to wear over his shoulder.

Piggy Bank Gonzales couldn't
get close enough to choose one.

Again the pigs made him dance
until the bill was paid.

A man came by selling ices.
"I want strawberry,"
said one of the pigs.

"I like cherry," said another.

"Do you have any pineapple?"
asked a third.

Piggy Bank Gonzales
was going to ask for grape.
But he never got the chance.

"That was very refreshing,"
said the pigs,
smacking their lips.

The man held out his hand
for his money.

The musicians played.
Piggy Bank Gonzales danced.

He danced and he danced
and he danced.

But there were no more coins.
The piggy bank was empty.

"We can't pay you," said the pigs.

The man was angry.
"Robbers!" he shouted.
"I'll teach you
to cheat an old man!"
And he chased them with a stick.

"It's all YOUR fault!"
the pigs shouted
at Piggy Bank Gonzales
as they ran off and left him.
They were soon out of sight.

Piggy Bank Gonzales had short legs.
He could not run very fast.
"If the man hits me with that stick
I'll break!" he thought.

Just in time he hid among some pots.
The man could not find him.

After a while the man gave up
and went away.

Piggy Bank Gonzales ran home
as fast as he could.

Once again the piggy bank's life
was quiet and comfortable
and not very exciting.

"Just the way I like it,"
said Piggy Bank Gonzales.